MW00878194

Copyright: Published in the United States
by Nona J. Fairfax / © Nona J. Fairfax

Published 02/02/2015

Little Girl and the Ponies
Book 1

Introduction

For many parents, curling up with a book for a bedtime story with their kid is a daily ritual. For others, it is the perfect time to spend time with their children after a busy day, and for some, it is something they should do but are not entirely sure why. Discover these benefits of bedtime stories for kids.

Sharpen their brains

Research shows that one of the greatest benefit of interacting with children, including reading to them stories, is that children learn a great deal of things- from improved logic skills to lowering their stress levels. Bedtime stories rewire the brain of a child and quicken their mastery of language. Their vocabulary repertoire is expanded and their listening and oral communication skills enhanced.

Enhance creativity and Stimulate imagination

If you are a good storyteller, then you should teleport your kid to a different realm- from reality to fantasy for the child to learn the difference between these two. This will enhance and stimulate his imagination.

Emotion development

The kid will learn to experience different emotions while empathizing with the characters of the story. The common emotions of sadness, happiness and anger may be encountered and he will learn to control these in real life.

Content

7 Tips to Help Ignite Your Child's Imagination

Imagination, often the concept we associate with joy, whimsy, and play, is just as easily involving cognitive capability, logical reasoning, and mental stability. The process the brain goes through when utilizing make-believe notions is a mixture of curiosity, adrenaline, and the practicing of creativity and exploration of different ideas previously unreached. Doing so exercises several parts of the adolescent mind, and will be reflected upon in the future, by means of open-mindedness, reason, and the ability to fathom abstractions above and beyond that of the average mind.

By incorporating these tips and activities into the lifestyles of both you and your child, your pudgy genius will not only be more mentally efficient, but happier and more capable overall.

1.   Ask Boggling Questions
       Parents tend to underestimate the span of their child's intelligence, restraining their capacity. Ask questions that are "out of the box", for instance, "what do you think that toad is thinking?" or "how come the clouds are floating?" Questions that you wouldn't normally consider completely sane, probably absurd to the outside world, can be awe-inspiring and full of wonder to your child, opening doors of imagination and invention in their minds. In addition, try to respond to their answers with "why do you think that is?" or "how can you tell?", thereby teaching them that questions are meant to be explored, and ideas full of possibility. Most importantly, never allow your child to say "I don't know". Teach them that your questions have no right answer, as long as they make you think.

2.   Keep Questions Open-ended
       Steer clear of words such as "wrong" or "try again", which will force children to believe that questions can only have one answer, with strict guidelines and a sole truth. They will later apply this mantra to their everyday behavior, and think in a more linear format, essentially restricting their minds and ideas.

3.   Ask "what if?"
      What if trees could move? What if you your teacher were an ogre? What if giraffes could talk? Let your child explore things beyond the dimensions of reality, and allow them to conceive concepts far and wide.

4.   Tell Stories
      Pictures and imagery are unimportant, even less effective than simply speaking a story to your child. Use different voices, adjectives, and hand gestures when speaking, allowing your child to fill in the blanks of the story, creating a sort of movie in their own heads. Unlike in TV, in stories, children do not have their visuals presented to them. Make these epic narratives engaging, and allow your child to add to the story. This will open the door to creative writing, as well as reading and extensive thought. It is so important to constantly exercise your child's mind, allowing it to be flexible and thrive in mentally straining instances in adulthood.

5.   Create Art
Allow your child to openly explore their artistic talent. By letting your child draw, paint, or simply create the ideas in their minds, you are solidifying the concepts they invent, giving them meaning and allowing them to come to life. Even if their drawing capabilities are short of Mozart material, by creating art, your child will learn to express his or herself, perhaps opening up new areas of interest.

You can create hand puppets, form houses out of old packing boxes, or have fun with finger paints. The expanse of art is endlessly vast, and it's fine simply to explore its plains.

6. Encourage Openness

In addition to openness regarding the imagination, encourage trying new things. Whether this is varying foods, different school clubs, and even new friendships, your child can experience anything from an engaging hobby to understanding the conditions of friendship. Moreover, try not to overly shelter your child. Children who understand death at an early age will better cope with it in the future, and adolescents familiar with financial instability will learn from their parent's experiences and be more understanding and compassionate toward adversity. Of course, there is a period in childhood when not to be too open, just keep in mind that hiding everything from your child is not realistic nor healthy.

7.   Leave Room for Growth

A flower doesn't bloom under watch, and a child's imagination cannot grow in a cramped environment. Allow him or her space to explore the world. Let your child establish independence, while still maintaining the assurance of an adult figure, in case things go astray. It's often hard to let go of your child, and that's OK, however it's imperative to refrain from being overly invasive, as this will likely cause your child to become dependent and create a barricade between them and their full capacity.

Little Girl and the Ponies

Kira lived with her parents in a city. She went to a good school, and had good marks. Eight year old Kira was not feeling well today, so her mama made her skip school, and even she did not go to work.

Kira, like every girl, loved pink. She had a pink room; all of her furniture, and her bed, and her drapes were pink in color. She had all kinds of plush animals, and among all her favorite was her pink horse, which she had named Kelly. Kelly was a light pink colored plush horse, with big, darker colored eye lids with long eye lashes. She had a long, white, mane that fell across her ears on the top of her head, and a long, white tail. Kelly was so special that Kira kept her beside her every second of the day.

Kira's mama made her a hot bowl of soup, and asked her to take a nap.

"Sleep, baby, so your fever will go away," she said, as she tucked Kira into her bed.

"Mama, please give Kelly to me; I want to sleep with her. I have beautiful dreams when Kelly sleeps with me," said Kira.

"Sure, baby," said her mama. Kelly was on the shelf at the moment, but as her mother pulled Kelly down, her tail came off in Kira's mama's hand.

"Oh no, Mama, Kelly is hurt; her tail came off!" said Kira with a fright.

"It's ok, honey, while you sleep, mama will sew it back on," said her mama. She tucked Kira in, and soon Kira was fast asleep.

Kira woke up from her sleep to see that above her was a pink cloud, and as her eyes stared at this, a flash of lightning struck her. Kira fainted. She woke up after a few hours to find that she was in a different land. Kira tried to sit up. Around her there were many ponies and horses looking down at her. She recognized one horse.

"Kelly, is that you?" she asked.

"Yes, Princess Kira! Are you all right?" asked Kelly.

"You can talk?" asked Kira in shock as she stood up.

"Of course. I'm a princess; we are in horse land, and we are in great danger, but the fairy god of our land has sent for you to rescue us," said Kelly. Kelly gave her neck to Kira to hold as she was standing up.

"Where is mama? Where is this place?" she asked, and she noticed something. "Where are all your tails?"

None of the horses had any tails.

"That is the problem we are facing, Princess. Your mother, our fairy god, is trying hard to fix it, but she needs your help; that is why she asked you to come help us," said Kelly. She looked so beautiful, but with her tail gone now, she looked incomplete. So did all of the other horses. They all looked so sad. I must help them, she made up her mind. She would do whatever it took to get the horses their tails back.

"Ride with me, Princess. I'll take you to your palace. We shall talk about the rescue plan in there; it's getting hot out here," said Kelly. Kira rode with Kelly to the palace.

As they rode to the palace, many horses and ponies came out of their homes to see her. They all knelt down in respect. She waved her hand across everybody were so thrilled to see her. She walked across a small town the whole town was made out of hay and stems. There were fields of carrots growing all around the town. Soon they reached a huge palace, and the whole palace was pink in color. As they walked in, Kira saw everything was in pink and white – long, white walls and shiny white floors, pink windows, and soft, satin, pink curtains. The furniture was also pink. There were many butler horses, who offered her sparkly water, and amazing looking snacks. Kelly led her into a long hallway. There was a throne in the center. The walls in this hall were lined with pictures. Most of them were of many young girls about her age. All of them were dressed in bright pink. The last frame was empty.

"Why does this frame not have a picture? Who are all these girls?" she asked.

"These are the princesses who came and rescued us during our bad times. This frame belongs to you; as soon as you rescue our tails, your picture will be up on the wall, just like the other princesses," said Kelly.

Kira felt greatly honored upon hearing that.

"Don't worry, Kelly, I'll save you! Now, please tell me what happened to your tail."

Kelly began to tell the story from the beginning. "There was a witch who came in as a poor beggar. The horses took pity on her, and made her stay with them, giving the witch food and a warm place to sleep. Soon the witch showed her true colors; she first nabbed all of the foals, one by one, and chopped their tails off. She soon fooled and tricked the whole village, and caught a hold of all of the ponies and horses, and took their tails off. I was the last one she could get her hands on."

"But how could you let her cut off your tail, Kelly? You are such a strong horse!" said Kira.

"She grew stronger with every tail she got from the horses. She used magic to trick us so she could cut them off of us," said Kelly, as she began to cry.

"There, there, Kelly; please, do tell me – why does she need your tail?"

"The evil witch is going to turn us all into donkeys. She is going to cast a spell using all of our tails to control us. Once we turn into donkeys, we will be her slaves forever!" Kelly burst into tears. She cried aloud.

"I won't let her do that! I will save you, Kelly. Now tell me your plan," said Kira taking leadership.

"Thank you, Princess. Right now, your mother is struggling to get our tails back. You must trick the witch so that she will not be able to finish her spell, and if we are in time, your mother our fairy queen, will stitch the tails back, and all our lives will be saved," said Kelly. Kira have Kelly a big hug and whipped her tears.

That night, Kelly took Kira to the witch's lair. From the outside, Kira could hear the chanting of the witch, and she thought, she must be saying her spell. Kira had no time to lose. She had to fool the witch until her mother had enough time to stick the tails back on. She was scared, but the thought of Kelly made her brave. She first ran to the storage area, where she found some empty containers. The witch must have used them all to cast the spell, and kept the tails here, she thought.

The containers were double her size. Kira pushed them, but they didn't move. She used a long rod in the corner as a lever, and that worked; the containers that had been piled up, fell over and onto each other, making a lot of noise. Kira ducked so she would not get hurt, and hid behind a wall. The witch was distracted by the noise, so she came out to check if the horses were creating a mess. Kira took the chance and moved out quickly, as the witch was looking into the storage room. Next, Kira saw a large drape separating the chamber and the other room. She climbed on top of it carefully. She used a knife that she was carrying with her to cut off the sides of the drape. As she did, she heard the witch stomping back. Kira quickly slid down the large drape. She found a pillar and hid behind it. The witch walked right through the drape, but when the witch pushed it back, the drape fell on her. Kira had torn it at just the right angle. The witch struggled with the heavy drape on top of her. Looking at this opportunity, Kira whistled loudly. Kelly and her other friends ran into the room. They jumped all over the tangled witch, stamping on her, and kicking her hard. Kira ran to the center, where the witch was chanting. She broke the wand, which had landed on the floor. The witch lost all of her powers. She saw her mother, the fairy queen of the house land, rescue all of the tails. Magically, the horses got their tails back. It all happened thanks to the bravery of Princess Kira. The fairy queen waved her wand across the witch and made her disappear forever. All the horses thanked the fairy queen as she vanished.

Kira rode back to the palace with Kelly, who was now galloping with joy because of getting her beautiful tail back.

As soon as she entered the palace, Kira saw her picture was in the frame that had been empty before. Kira was now one of the official PINK PRINCESSES since she had saved the horses. Kira was invited to sit on the throne. All of the horses bowed to her, in return of her favor.

"It's time for you to go back," said Kelly.

"Oh no, Kelly, I just started to enjoy this place," said Kira.

"I know, Princess, but you have to go back to the human world. Don't worry, you'll have me with you there forever. Thank you, once again, for the bravery you showed, Princess," Kelly thanked her.

Soon the pink cloud came over her again, and flashed a lightning bolt.

Kira woke up in her bed. Her mother sat beside her, holding her favorite toy, Kelly.

"Oh Mama, you fixed her tail! Thank you so much," said Kira hugging her mama tightly.

"I couldn't have done it without your help, baby," said her mama, as she kissed her on her forehead.

Kira looked at Kelly, and her tail; she looked so beautiful with her tail back on. She kissed Kelly on her head.

THE END.

ABOUT AUTHOR

Nona J. Fairfax.

Nona J. Fairfax is an accomplished storybook author that has a strong passion for writing when it comes to improving the lives of children. She has a strong sense of pride for her work, and continues to thrive for a more universal world that keeps children and families in the foremost front of her mind. Her life's work includes writing children's books that help to improve the parent-child relationship, bedtime stories, and smaller pieces of art. When she is not busy writing about improving the lives of children.

MY BEST SELLER ON AMAZON

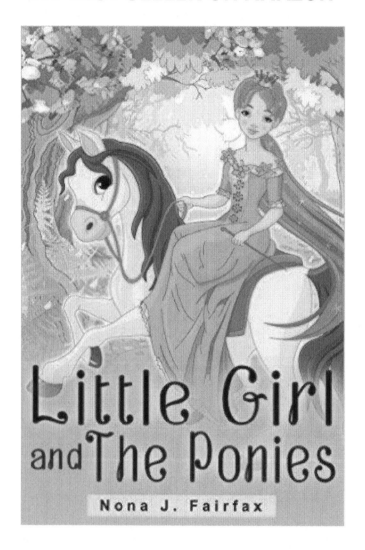

Download on:
www.amazon.com/dp/B00S2V6Z1W

Download on:
www.amazon.com/dp/ B00Y5DC4MU

Download on:
www.amazon.com/dp/B00Z7CJI72

Download on:
www.amazon.com/dp/ B00YL3PJSK

Download on:
www.amazon.com/dp/B010LP0TJU

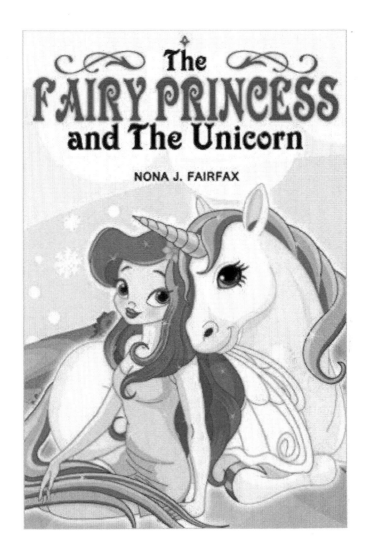

Download on:
www.amazon.com/dp/ B00WXI5HDM

Made in the USA
Middletown, DE
09 December 2016